When I Grow Up...
Builder

Written by Clare Hibbert
Illustrated by Mike Byrne

Consultant: Jason Walker

LADYBIRD BOOKS

UK | USA | Canada | Ireland | Australia
India | New Zealand | South Africa

Ladybird Books is part of the Penguin Random House group of companies
whose addresses can be found at global.penguinrandomhouse.com.

ladybird.com

Penguin
Random House
UK

First published 2016
001

Printed in China

A CIP catalogue record for this book is available from the British Library

ISBN: 978-0-723-29471-9

Contents

What do builders do?

Being a builder is an important job. Builders make and repair buildings that we use every day. Look at some of the things they do.

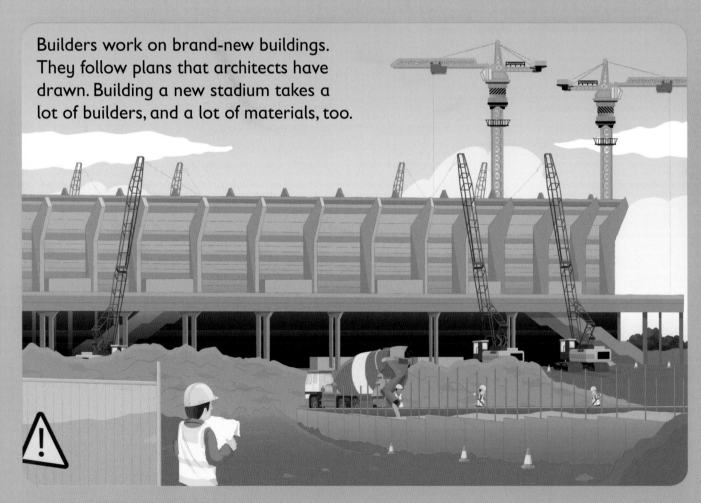

Builders work on brand-new buildings. They follow plans that architects have drawn. Building a new stadium takes a lot of builders, and a lot of materials, too.

Builders improve existing buildings.
They can even make them bigger.
This house is having an extra
room added at the back.

Builders repair old buildings. Over the years,
roofs, walls and foundations can be damaged.
Builders repair them so they stand strong
and look good.

On the building site

A building site is where a big building project takes place. Lots of builders work on the site for weeks, months or even years.

This is the site office, where the site manager works. Her job is to make sure the building is finished safely and on time.

Daily life

Many different things go on at the building site each day. Builders use different machines and tools to carry out their jobs.

Builders use a bulldozer to make the plot as flat as possible.

Builders mix cement and water in a concrete mixer to make concrete.

Delivery trucks bring in timber, plasterboard and other building materials.

Bricklayers build solid walls using large breeze blocks.

Metalworkers use nuts and bolts to put together a building's steel frame.

Dressed for work

Builders must dress safely for the job they do. They need to stand out on a busy site and be well protected when using machines and tools.

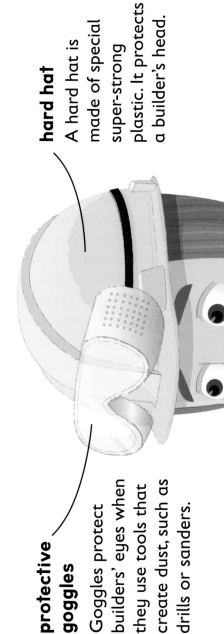

hard hat
A hard hat is made of special super-strong plastic. It protects a builder's head.

walkie-talkie
Builders carry a walkie-talkie to communicate with others around the site.

protective goggles
Goggles protect builders' eyes when they use tools that create dust, such as drills or sanders.

hi-vis vest
A high-visibility jacket makes builders easy to spot.

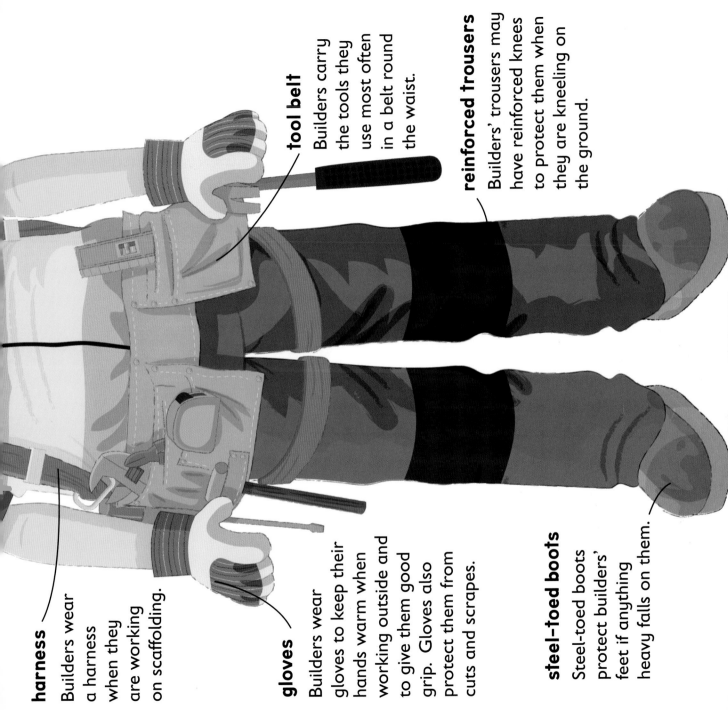

harness
Builders wear a harness when they are working on scaffolding.

gloves
Builders wear gloves to keep their hands warm when working outside and to give them good grip. Gloves also protect them from cuts and scrapes.

tool belt
Builders carry the tools they use most often in a belt round the waist.

reinforced trousers
Builders' trousers may have reinforced knees to protect them when they are kneeling on the ground.

steel-toed boots
Steel-toed boots protect builders' feet if anything heavy falls on them.

11

Builder's toolbox

A builder's toolbox has lots of space for all the tools he needs, both big and small. The box has handy compartments to store everything.

Builders carry their tools to each building site they work on. This toolbox has wheels to make it easy to move around.

nails

trowel

spanner

safety goggles

pencil

screwdriver

knife

set square

tape measure

Multi-cutter

Builders can change the attachment of this tool to cut, sand or scrape.

Nail gun

This is used to firmly fix nails into wood or other hard materials.

Grinder

This powerful tool is used by builders to cut through metal.

Wood planer

Builders use this to flatten or shape large pieces of wood.

Impact wrench

This tool quickly tightens and unscrews nuts and bolts.

Rivet gun

Builders use this to join two pieces of metal together.

Tools for the job

Without tools, builders couldn't do their jobs. Tools make the work easier and more accurate, but they must be used safely.

Cordless drill

This makes holes for screws and bolts. It can be used anywhere because it runs off batteries.

Sander

This is used to smooth down wood and other surfaces. A builder wears goggles and a mask while sanding because it creates a lot of dust.

Battery-operated saw

This saw uses batteries so a builder can cut different materials without a power cord getting in the way.

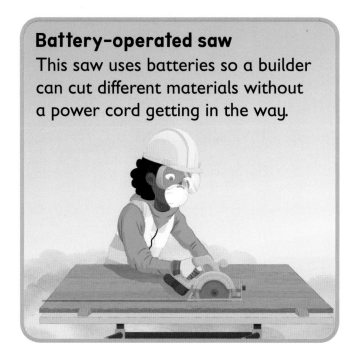

Demolition hammer

This solid metal hammer can break through walls.

Spirit level

This helps a bricklayer make sure walls, shelves and other things are straight.

Concrete breaker

This breaks through roads or pavements.

New homes

Builders can transform a bare patch of land into homes for families. First, an architect comes up with the drawings and plans.

The builders mark where the foundations will go so the digger driver knows where to dig.

The builders pour concrete into the foundations from a huge lorry.

The bricklayers build the walls. These have two layers —
an outside wall of bricks, and an inside wooden framework.

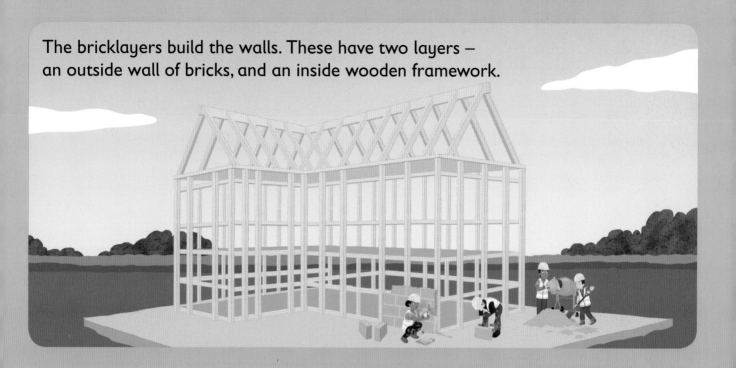

The roofers make a timber framework for the roof, then nail on the roof tiles.

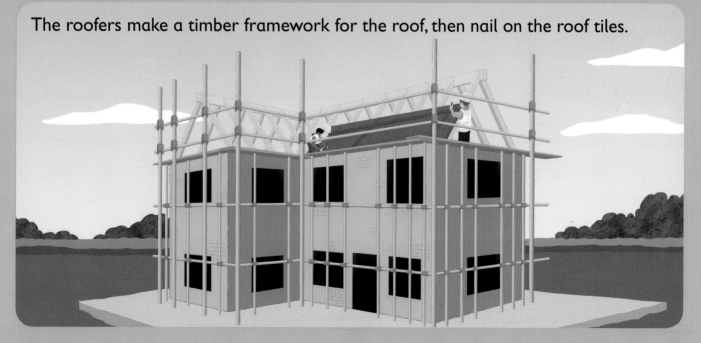

Pulling down buildings

Most of the time, builders are busy putting up new structures. Sometimes, though, they must do the complete opposite – pull them down!

Wrecking ball
This old house is being knocked down with a wrecking ball. This heavy ball swings from a crane and bashes against the walls.

Explosives

Explosives have been put into the walls of this tower block. When they detonate, the building will collapse in seconds.

Robotic demolition

Builders use remote-controlled robots to pull down some buildings. The machines move on rubber tracks and are fitted with jaw-like crushers.

Moving machines

There are lots of different vehicles on a building site. Some have caterpillar tracks, which grip well in the mud, instead of wheels.

Crane

This is for lifting heavy objects very high. The lifting arm is called the jib.

Forklift truck

This moves small loads, such as pallets of bricks, around the building site.

Excavator

This digs earth out of the ground with its bucket, which is on the end of a moving arm.

Backhoe loader

This has a large bucket at the end of its arm. It moves and carries materials such as gravel and rubble.

Concrete-mixer truck

This truck mixes the concrete and then pours it out of a chute.

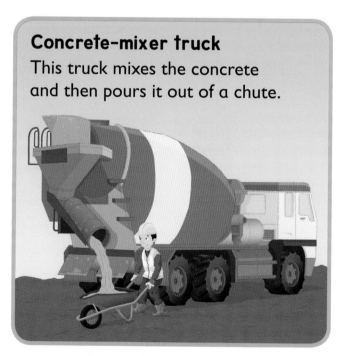

Bulldozer

This has a big steel blade at the front for moving mounds of soil, bricks or rubbish.

Working together

Builders work on projects with other experts. Everyone has their own special skills and knowledge to help finish off buildings.

Plumber

A plumber fits the water pipes and waste pipes and then puts in toilets, sinks, showers and baths.

Electrician

An electrician does the electrical wiring that powers the sockets and light fittings in the whole house.

Plasterer

The plasterer smooths plaster over the bare breeze blocks to create nice flat walls.

Decorators

Painters and decorators paint or wallpaper the walls and ceilings.

Joiner

A joiner fits special wooden parts like the stairs and banisters.

Carpenter

A carpenter makes and fits interior parts like doors and cupboards.

Bridges, tunnels and roads

Specialists called civil engineers build bridges, roads and tunnels. Making them safe is a very important job.

Bridges are built to carry people, cars or trains over a gap, such as a river or a valley. The top part that people go across is called the deck. This bridge is a suspension bridge – the deck hangs from special cables.

A tunnel takes a road or railway through a mountain, underground or under the sea. Builders use an enormous drill, called a boring machine, to build a tunnel.

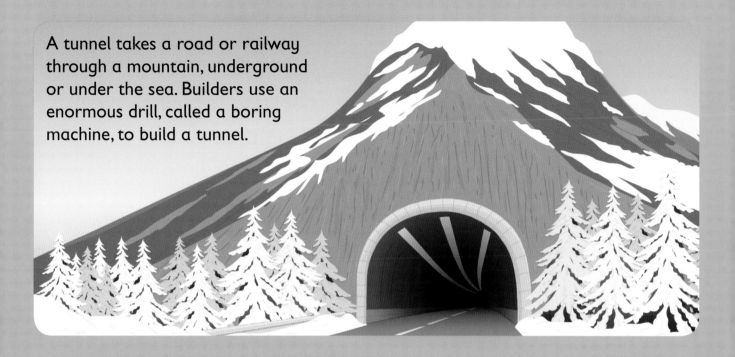

Junctions are built so cars can move smoothly from road to road. Places where many roads meet, crossing over and under each other, are nicknamed spaghetti junctions – because they look like a big bowl of spaghetti!

Around the world

Thoughout history, people have built awe-inspiring structures. Here are some of the world's most famous buildings.

The Great Pyramid

The Great Pyramid was built 4,500 years ago at Giza, in Egypt. It stands 146 metres high.

The Leaning Tower of Pisa

This tower in Italy took 200 years to build, but it is not straight! Luckily it has now stopped tilting.

The Colosseum

Some parts of this ancient Roman theatre fell down over the years due to earthquakes.

The Sydney Opera House

This concert hall in Australia has roofs that look like sails or choppy waves.

The Gherkin

This skyscraper office building in London, in the UK, is nicknamed the Gherkin.

Burj Khalifa

This skyscraper in Dubai is the world's tallest building. It stands 829.9 metres high.

Traditional homes

For years, people have traditionally used a range of different materials and styles for their buildings.

In hot parts of Africa and the Middle East, people bake mud in the sun to make bricks.

The Toda people of southern India build their homes from bamboo. They use grass to thatch the roof.

Near pine forests, people build homes from timber. A pointed roof lets rain and snow slide off.

Traditional Japanese homes are made of wood, with inside walls of bamboo and mud.

The Uros people live on Lake Titicaca, high up in the Andes Mountains of South America. They use reeds from the lake to build their homes.

Being a good builder

Being a builder is very hard work. It is not a job for everyone. To be good at the job, you need certain qualities.

Builders have to be fit and strong. They are always on the go, carrying heavy things or using heavy machinery.

Builders need to be able to turn an architect's plans into reality. They must pay attention to details, but have imagination, too!

Builders need to have brilliant coordination. They need to stay in control when operating complicated heavy machinery.

Builders need to be good at maths and working things out. They must measure spaces and order enough building materials.

Glossary

architect   Someone who designs buildings and produces plans that builders follow.

breeze block   A large brick made of concrete.

caterpillar tracks   A belt that moves round a vehicle's wheels, for example a bulldozer's, giving it a good grip on rough ground.

civil engineer   Someone who designs, builds and looks after big structures like bridges, roads and tunnels.

detonate   To set off an explosion.

explosive   A substance that can make things blow up.

foundations   The base that a building stands on, usually made by filling holes or trenches with concrete.

scaffolding   Poles and planks that form a framework around a building and that builders can stand on while they are working up high.

spirit level   A tube of glass that contains a bubble of air trapped inside it. Builders know that, when the bubble is in the middle, the spirit level is resting on something exactly flat or level.